Here's what kids have to say about reading Magic Tree House® books and Magic Tree House® Merlin Missions:

Thank you for writing these great books! I have learned a great deal of information about history and the world around me.—Rosanna

Your series, the Magic Tree House, was really influential on my late childhood years. [Jack and Annie] taught me courage through their rigorous adventures and profound friendship, and how they stuck it out through thick and thin, from start to finish.—Joe

Your description is fantastic! The words pop out . . . oh, man . . . [the Magic Tree House series] is really exciting!—Christina

I like the Magic Tree House series. I stay up all night reading them. Even on school nights!—Peter

I think I've read about twenty-five of your Magic Tree House books! I'm reading every Magic Tree House book I can get my hands on!—Jack

Never stop writing, and if you can't think about anything to write about, don't worry, use some of my ideas!!—Kevin

Parents, teachers, and librarians love Magic Tree House® books, too!

[Magic Tree House] comes up quite a bit at parent/ teacher conferences. . . . The parents are amazed at how much more reading is being done at home because of your books. I am very pleased to know such fun and interesting reading exists for students. . . . Your books have also made students want to learn more about the places Jack and Annie visit. What wonderful starters for some research projects! —Kris L.

As a librarian, I have seen many happy young readers coming into the library to check out the next Magic Tree House book in the series. I have assisted young library patrons with finding nonfiction materials related to the Magic Tree House book they have read. . . . The message you are sending to children is invaluable: siblings can be friends; boys and girls can hang out together. . . . —Lynne H.

[My daughter] had a slow start reading, but somehow with your Magic Tree House series, she has been inspired and motivated to read. It is with such urgency that she tracks down your books. She often blurts out various facts and lines followed by "I read that in my Magic Tree House book." —Jenny E.

[My students] seize every opportunity they can to reread a Magic Tree House book or look at all the wonderful illustrations. Jack and Annie have opened a door to a world of literacy that I know will continue throughout the lives of my students.—Deborah H.

[My son] carries his Magic Tree House books everywhere he goes. He just can't put the book he is reading down until he finishes it. . . . He is doing better in school overall since he has made reading a daily thing. He even has a bet going with his aunt that if he continues doing well in school, she will continue to buy him the next book in the Magic Tree House series.—Rosalie R.

MAGIC TREE HOUSE® #35
A MERLIN MISSION

Night of the New Magicians

by Mary Pope Osborne

illustrated by Sal Murdocca

A STEPPING STONE BOOK™

Random House 🏠 New York

Text copyright © 2006 by Mary Pope Osborne
Illustrations copyright © 2006 by Sal Murdocca
Window cling illustration copyright © 2006 by Sal Murdocca

Published in the United States by Random House Children's Books, a division of Random House, Inc., New York. Originally published in hardcover by Random House Children's Books, a division of Random House, Inc., in 2006.

RANDOM HOUSE and colophon are registered trademarks and A STEPPING STONE BOOK and colophon are trademarks of Random House, Inc. MAGIC TREE HOUSE is a registered trademark of Mary Pope Osborne; used under license.

www.randomhouse.com/kids
www.magictreehouse.com

Educators and librarians, for a variety of teaching tools, visit us at
www.randomhouse.com/teachers

Library of Congress Cataloging-in-Publication Data
Osborne, Mary Pope.
Night of the new magicians / by Mary Pope Osborne ; illustrated by Sal Murdocca.
   p.   cm. — (Magic tree house ; #35)
"A Merlin mission."
"A Stepping Stone book."
SUMMARY: Jack and Annie visit the Paris World's Fair of 1889 in an effort to protect four scientific pioneers from an evil sorcerer.
ISBN 978-0-375-83035-8 (trade) — ISBN 978-0-375-93035-5 (lib. bdg.) —
ISBN 978-0-375-83036-5 (pbk.)
1. Exposition universelle de 1889 (Paris, France)—Juvenile fiction. [1. Paris World's Fair (1889)—Fiction. 2. Time travel—Fiction. 3. Magic—Fiction. 4. Brothers and sisters—Fiction. 5. Science—Fiction. 6. Paris (France)—History—1870–1940—Fiction.
7. France—History—Third Republic, 1870–1940—Fiction.] I. Murdocca, Sal, ill. II. Title. III. Series: Osborne, Mary Pope. Magic tree house series ; #35.
PZ7.O81167Nhu   2006   [Fic]—dc22   2005018280

Printed in the United States of America
20 19

To Joe Alicata, Magician of Design

Dear Reader,

For years I've wanted Jack and Annie to travel to one of my favorite cities in the world—Paris, France. Finally, one day, while doing some research, I came across the perfect setting for a Paris adventure: the Exposition Universelle, 1889—or, as it's otherwise known, the Paris World's Fair of 1889. In the years before air travel, television, and the Internet, people attended world's fairs to learn about the food, dress, and customs of other cultures. They also saw exhibitions of the newest machines and inventions.

During the late 1800s, the world was experiencing great technological change—even greater change than our world today. Join Jack and Annie as they set out on a dangerous mission to that wondrous time. . . .

Mary Pope Osborne

CONTENTS

Clear-eyed Science and active Industry
Have erected, among the spacious palaces,
An iron Tower leading to the heavens.
—from *The Song of the Century*
by the *Comédie Française*

Prologue

One summer day, a mysterious tree house appeared in the woods. A brother and sister named Jack and Annie soon learned that the tree house was magic—it could take them to any time and any place in history. They also learned that the tree house belonged to Morgan le Fay, a magical librarian from the legendary realm of Camelot.

After Jack and Annie traveled on many adventures for Morgan, Merlin the magician began sending them on "Merlin Missions" in the tree house. With help from two young sorcerers named Teddy and Kathleen, Jack and Annie visited four mythical places and found valuable objects to help save Camelot.

For their next four Merlin Missions, Jack and Annie were told they must travel to *real* times and *real* places in history and prove to Merlin that they could use magic wisely. First they went on a mission to the city of Venice, and then they journeyed to the ancient city of Baghdad. Now they are waiting to hear from Merlin again. . . .

CHAPTER ONE

Four New Magicians

Jack sat on the porch, reading in the summer twilight. Crickets chirped in the Frog Creek woods. The bell of an ice cream truck jingled down the street.

Annie stepped out the front door. "Let's go," she said.

"Where?" said Jack.

"Mom gave us money for ice cream," said Annie.

"Cool," said Jack. He pulled on his backpack. Then he followed Annie down the porch steps.

As they headed up the sidewalk, the smell of damp leaves and moss wafted from the woods.

Annie stopped walking. "Listen," she said.

Jack listened. "What?" he said. "I don't hear anything."

"That's the *point*," said Annie. "A minute ago, the crickets were blaring away. Now everything's super quiet."

Jack listened again. Annie was right. All the Frog Creek woods seemed to be holding its breath.

"Do you think . . . ?" said Jack.

"Maybe," said Annie, grinning. "Let's go check!"

Jack and Annie hurried across the street and into the dimly lit woods. They walked quickly between the leafy trees, until they came to the tallest oak. A rope ladder dangled from the tree-top. The magic tree house sat high in the branches, catching the last light of day.

Jack smiled. "I guess ice cream will have to wait," he said.

"Yep," said Annie. She grabbed the ladder and climbed up. Jack climbed up after her.

Inside the tree house, dusky light filtered through the window. Lying on the wooden floor was a folded piece of paper and a slim book with a red cover.

Annie grabbed the paper. Jack picked up the book. "This must be a research book from Morgan," he said.

The book's title was written in gold letters:

Guide Book:
Paris World's Fair
~1889~

"Paris World's Fair?" said Jack.

"That sounds like fun!" said Annie.

"Yeah, but I wonder why we're going there," said Jack.

"This should tell us," said Annie. She unfolded the paper. "It's Merlin's handwriting." She read aloud:

To Jack and Annie of Frog Creek:
I have discovered that an evil sorcerer is plotting to steal the secrets of four new magicians at the Paris World's Fair.

Your mission is to find the magicians, warn them, and learn their secrets for me. The four new magicians are:

The Magician of Sound—
his voice can be heard
for a thousand miles.

The Magician of Light—
his fires glow,
but they do not burn.

The Magician of the Invisible—
he battles deadly enemies
no one can see.

The Magician of Iron—

he bends the metals of earth
and triumphs over the wind.

Good luck,
M.

"Our mission sounds more like a fairy tale than real life," said Jack. "An evil sorcerer. Magicians of the Invisible, Light, Sound, and Iron. They sound like they belong in a magical place like Camelot, not a real place like Paris, France."

"But we're going to a World's Fair," said Annie. "That sounds kind of magical, doesn't it?"

"Maybe," said Jack. "But why do such powerful magicians need our help in the first place? Why can't they defeat the evil sorcerer with their own powers?"

"Maybe the sorcerer's power is stronger than theirs," said Annie.

"So maybe we can help them with Teddy and Kathleen's rhymes," said Jack.

Annie gasped. "Oh, no! We need the rhyme book! We have to go back home and get it!"

"Don't worry, I have it," said Jack. "Ever since we got back from Baghdad, I've been taking it with me everywhere I go—just in case Merlin sends for us."

"Whew," said Annie. "Let's take a look."

Jack reached into his backpack. He pulled out the small book written by their two young sorcerer friends from Camelot:

**10 MAGIC RHYMES FOR ANNIE AND JACK
FROM TEDDY AND KATHLEEN**

Jack turned to the table of contents. "Okay, we've used five rhymes on our last two missions," he said. "So we have five left for the next two. We haven't used *Spin into the Air*, or *Make Something Disappear*, or *Pull a Cloud from the*

Sky, or *Find a Treasure You Must Never Lose,* or *Turn into Ducks.*"

"Quack! Quack!"

Jack looked up.

"Just kidding," said Annie.

"You'd better not make jokes about these rhymes," Jack said. "You might end up saying the wrong one at the wrong time and really get us in trouble." He closed the rhyme book. "Ready to go?"

"Ready," said Annie.

Jack took a deep breath and picked up the guide book to the 1889 Paris World's Fair. He pointed to the title. "I wish we could go there," he said.

The wind started to blow.

The tree house started to spin.

It spun faster and faster.

Then everything was still.

Absolutely still.

CHAPTER TWO

A Living Encyclopedia

Jack opened his eyes. The scent of roses floated through the warm twilight. Jack was wearing an old-fashioned cap, a rust-colored jacket, and knee-length pants. His backpack had turned into a leather satchel.

Annie was wearing a puffy white blouse and a long purple skirt with a ruffle. "Look, there's the Eiffel Tower," she said.

Jack looked. They had landed in a park filled with trees. Beyond the park, rising into the sky, was a tall tower with lights beaming from the top.

"That's the Eiffel Tower, all right," said Jack.

"But where's the World's Fair?" He opened their guide book and found a map. "Oh, great, it looks like the fair is directly below the tower. That should make it easy to find."

"Let's get going," said Annie.

"Wait, we need to go over what we have to do on our mission," said Jack.

"It's simple," said Annie. "We have to find the Magician of Sound, the Magician of Light, the Magician of the Invisible, and the Magician of Iron. We have to warn them about the evil sorcerer and then learn their secrets for Merlin."

"That doesn't sound simple to me," said Jack. "It sounds like a huge responsibility."

"So we'd better start *now*," said Annie. "Come on." Annie led the way down the tree house ladder.

Jack put their World's Fair guide into his satchel, along with their letter from Merlin and the book of rhymes from Teddy and Kathleen.

Then he followed Annie down the ladder.

As Jack and Annie started across the park, a clinking sound came from Annie's skirt pocket. She reached into the pocket and pulled out a handful of coins. "Hey, our ice cream money got changed into French coins!" she said.

"Good," said Jack. "We might need them at the fair."

Jack and Annie followed a gravel path that led out of the park and onto an avenue lit by gas streetlamps. Horse-drawn carriages and old-fashioned bicycles clattered over the cobblestones. They all seemed to be headed toward a crowded bridge that crossed a wide river.

Boats were gliding down the river, their lights reflecting in the water. On the far side of the river, thousands of tiny lamps twinkled along the bank. The Eiffel Tower glowed in the silver twilight.

"Paris is so beautiful," said Annie.

"No kidding," said Jack. "Let's cross that

bridge to the fair." They hurried to join the people streaming across the bridge.

Jack and Annie blended in easily with the happy crowd. The kids in the crowd were all wearing clothes like theirs. Most of the men wore black top hats and black coats and pants. The women wore hats as big as flower baskets. Their long, colorful dresses puffed out in back.

There seemed to be visitors from many countries. Jack saw Chinese straw hats, Dutch caps, several Indian turbans, and a Mexican sombrero.

"This reminds me of the carnival we went to in Venice," said Annie.

"Me too," said Jack. "Except in Venice, people were wearing costumes. Here, they're wearing their real clothes. Remember, this is a *world's* fair."

"Cool," said Annie.

Jack looked around. How would they recognize the four new magicians? he wondered. Would they be dressed like people from Paris?

Or people from another country? Or would they look like Merlin or Morgan in flowing medieval robes? And what about the evil sorcerer?

"Looks like we buy our tickets over there," said Annie as they reached the end of the bridge.

Jack and Annie headed for a ticket booth near an entrance gate. Above the gate, a giant banner read:

Welcome to the 1889 Paris World's Fair

As they stood in line waiting to buy tickets, Jack pulled out their guide book. "We need to prepare for our mission," he said. He turned to the first page and read aloud:

> **Welcome to the World's Fair—a living encyclopedia with over 60,000 exhibits from all over the globe!**

"Maybe some of the exhibits are magic shows," said Annie. "And that's where we'll find the new magicians."

"Maybe," said Jack. He kept reading:

This World's Fair is a showcase of progress! Discover the genius of man! Learn all about science and technology! See wondrous new machines and inventions!

Jack looked up. "Hmm," he said. "It sounds like this fair is mainly about inventions and scientific stuff. I don't see anything here about magic or magicians."

"How many?" the ticket seller asked gruffly. They had reached the front of the line.

Annie held out a handful of French coins. "Two, please," she said.

The ticket seller took two coins. Annie put the remaining change back into her pocket. Then she and Jack walked through the gate into the 1889 Paris World's Fair.

CHAPTER THREE

Magic? Magicians?

"Wow," said Jack and Annie together.

Inside the crowded fairgrounds, below the looming Eiffel Tower, a band played a lively march. Fountains shot colored water high into the sky. A small train chugged through the crowd, blowing its whistle.

People of all ages from many different countries bustled about in the twilight. Everyone seemed to be having fun, reading from guide books, strolling from one exhibit to another, or buying refreshments and souvenirs.

"We can't see much from here," said Annie. "It's hard to know what's going on."

"What about that little train?" said Jack. "Maybe we could ride on it and get a good look at everything."

"Great idea," said Annie.

The train whistle blew again.

"Over there," said Jack. He pointed to a clear space where passengers were getting off the train and other passengers were boarding.

"Hurry!" said Jack.

They raced to the train and jumped on. Annie dug into her pocket and took out some coins. She held them out to the conductor. He took a few, and Jack and Annie squeezed into seats on a wooden bench. The whistle blew, steam sputtered out of the smokestack, and the small train began to move.

"Look for anything about magic or magicians," said Jack.

As the train slowly chugged through the

World's Fair, a tour guide's voice blared from a megaphone: "Welcome to the World's Fair Sightseeing Train! On your ride, you will witness the astounding history of human structures as seen nowhere else! In every age, buildings had style and beauty."

The train chugged by cave dwellings, canvas tents, and huts made of mud.

Magic? Magicians? Jack thought as he looked at the different structures. *No, no, no.*

The train passed a thatched cottage, a mansion with columns, and a palace with a huge golden dome.

No, no, no, Jack thought.

"Now we will visit the many lands of the world," said the tour guide. "First, Egypt!"

The train chugged past an outdoor café. Smells of grilled meat and rich coffee filled the air. Three women with veils over their faces danced to flute music.

No magicians there, thought Jack.

"Next we have an African village on the beautiful Serengeti Plain," said the tour guide. They
passed a cluster of huts surrounded by tall grass.
People played drums and shook gourd rattles.

Still no magicians, thought Jack.

"And now we visit a New Year's festival in faraway China," said the guide. The train chugged by Chinese acrobats and a huge dancing red dragon.

"Dragons are sort of magic, aren't they?" said Annie, looking back.

"It's just a couple of guys in a costume," said Jack. "That doesn't count."

"On our left is a Muslim mosque," the tour guide said. "On the right, a Buddhist temple. Here is an exquisite Japanese garden. . . ."

"No, no, no," murmured Jack.

The train passed by a show with dolls dressed in outfits from all around the world. It rolled by a giant brown statue of a woman. "This amazing creation is the Roman goddess Venus," said the tour guide, "made entirely of chocolate."

"That *is* amazing!" said Annie.

"It is, but it's not magic," said Jack.

The train rode by a globe of the world at least three stories high. The globe was turning slowly. "See the lovely mountains, deserts, rivers, and oceans of Earth," said the tour guide.

"This fair really *is* a living encyclopedia!" Annie said.

"But the encyclopedia doesn't have what we need to find," said Jack. He sighed and started thumbing through the guide book.

"Ahh, fantastic!" a train passenger said.

"Shocking!" said another.

"Magical!" exclaimed another.

Jack looked up. "Did someone just say *magical*?" he asked Annie.

"False alarm," said Annie. "They're talking about the Eiffel Tower."

The train came to a stop. All the passengers were gazing up. Pink lights lit the huge arches at the base of the tower.

"The Eiffel Tower was built especially for this World's Fair," said the tour guide. "The tower is nearly one thousand feet high, making it the tallest structure in the world today. Some of you may want to leave us here to get a closer look at Paris's newest miracle."

People began climbing off the train. "Maybe we should get off here, too," said Jack. "This train isn't much help."

Jack and Annie jumped off the train just

before its whistle blew and it started moving again.

"That's a tall tower," said Jack, looking up.

"*Really* tall," breathed Annie.

Iron rods rose in crisscross patterns high into the sky. Large elevators clanked up through the tower's lacy ironwork. Powerful spotlights beamed from the top of the tower, sweeping long fingers of light over the city.

"It would be fun to ride to the top in one of those elevators," said Annie.

"I know, but we don't have time," said Jack. "We have to find the four new magicians before the evil sorcerer finds them."

"I wonder if he's here yet," said Annie.

Jack and Annie looked around at all the people busily moving about the fairgrounds, going from one exhibit to another. Parents were holding their children's hands and pointing to the tower. Couples were strolling arm in arm. Everyone seemed happy and excited.

No one looks like an evil sorcerer, thought Jack. *No one looks like a Magician of Sound, or a Magician of Light, or a Magician of the Invisible, or a Magician of Iron, either.*

Jack's thoughts were interrupted by a young girl's voice—"You see, Papa? It is magic!"

"Magic?" said Jack. He and Annie looked at each other.

"Over there," said Annie. She pointed to a nearby exhibit. A little girl was laughing as her father pressed a pair of earpieces against his ears.

Jack and Annie walked closer to the exhibit. "It is positively unbelievable, Mimi!" the man said, shaking his head.

"It's magic, isn't it, Papa?" said the girl. "It can send a voice a thousand miles!"

Annie grabbed Jack's arm. "Did you hear what she just said?" she whispered. *"Send a voice a thousand miles*—that's what the Magician of Sound does!"

"Right!" said Jack. He and Annie looked at the sign above the exhibit. It said:

Telephone:
A New Invention by Alexander Graham Bell

"She's talking about a *telephone*!" said Jack. "I guess it's just been invented!"

"So Alexander Graham Bell must be the Magician of Sound!" said Annie.

"Oh, man, do you think Alexander Graham Bell is here in person?" said Jack.

"I'll ask," said Annie. She walked to a gray-haired woman helping with the exhibit. "Excuse me, but do you know where we can find Alexander Graham Bell?"

"I'm afraid he just left," said the woman.

"Where did he go?" asked Annie.

"I do not know," said the woman. "A strange man gave me an invitation to give to Mr. Bell. When Mr. Bell read it, he left at once. That is all I know. Excuse me." The woman turned away to answer someone else's question.

"Alexander Graham Bell!" Jack said to Annie. "He's a famous inventor, not a magician!"

"The evil sorcerer must've heard about the telephone and thought it was magic," said Annie.

"I wonder what that invitation said," said Jack. "And why did that lady say the messenger was strange?"

"Let's ask," said Annie.

Annie tapped the gray-haired woman on the arm. "Excuse me, we have two more questions," she said. "Do you know what was on the invitation? And why did you say the messenger was strange?"

"I do not know what the invitation said," replied the woman, "but the man who delivered it was dressed in a long, dark cloak. He wore a hood that hid most of his face, and he spoke in a deep, whispery voice."

Jack felt a chill go down his spine. *So that's what the evil sorcerer looks like,* he thought. *Just like you'd expect!*

"Sounds like the sorcerer," Annie whispered to Jack.

"I know, I know," Jack said, looking around.

"Do you have any idea where the strange

man in the cloak went?" Annie asked the woman.

"He asked for directions to the Hall of Machines," said the woman.

"Where's that?" asked Jack. "Is that here at the fair?"

"Yes, of course. It is the gigantic building made of glass. Can you see the roof?" The woman pointed to an arched glass rooftop looming above other fair buildings in the distance.

"I see it," said Annie.

"Good," said the woman. "Excuse me now. I must help some other people."

"Sure, thanks," said Annie. "Let's go," she said to Jack. She started walking quickly across the fairgrounds.

"Wait, wait, wait," said Jack, hurrying after her.

"The messenger is the sorcerer, I just know it!" said Annie.

"Of course he is," said Jack. "But what do we do when we find him?"

"I don't know yet," said Annie.

"He could be dangerous," said Jack. "We need to make a plan."

"We need to find him first," said Annie, "before he gets away! Hurry!" She broke into a run and dashed toward the Hall of Machines.

CHAPTER FOUR

Wizard of Menlo Park

Jack ran after Annie. He caught up to her outside the huge building made of glass. She was standing in line waiting to buy tickets.

"Listen," Jack said breathlessly, "we . . . we've got to make a plan. What if we suddenly find the sorcerer? What do we say to him? What if he tries to use his powers against us?"

"We use a rhyme," said Annie.

"Which rhyme?" said Jack.

"How many, children?" interrupted the ticket seller. They'd reached the front of the line.

"Two, please," said Annie, holding out some coins. The man gave her two tickets, and Annie turned back to Jack. "Let's go inside and see if we can find the sorcerer. Then we can figure out which rhyme."

"Okay, but be cool," said Jack, "so the sorcerer doesn't notice us."

Jack and Annie walked through the entrance of the glass building. "Oh, man," whispered Jack.

The Hall of Machines was the size of a football stadium. It was filled with thousands of people— and thousands of machines! Motors roared, wheels spun, gears clanked.

"What kind of place *is* this?" asked Annie.

Jack pulled out their guide book and read aloud:

> **In the Hall of Machines you will see machines from all over the world, bringing alive the world of engineers and inventors. You will see how cloth is sewn by machines to make clothes! You**

will see an exhibit of an automobile powered by gasoline! And of course, you will see a collection of inventions by the American grand-prize winner from Menlo Park, New Jersey—

"Look at that!" Annie interrupted. She pointed to a mechanical walkway overhead. The walkway circled the entire exhibit hall. Sightseers gazed down on all the exhibits. "We can get a look at everything from up there."

"Good," said Jack. "Maybe we can spot the sorcerer."

He put away the guide book and led the way up the stairs. They stepped onto the crowded moving walkway and peered down at all the people milling about the exhibit hall below.

There were lots of men dressed in black coats and top hats. There were American cowboys and bearded men in Arab robes and headcloths. But Jack didn't see a single scary-looking guy in a hooded cloak.

As Jack and Annie moved slowly over the exhibits, the air grew hotter and the sounds in the hall grew louder. Hammers hammered, sirens blew, bells rang, whistles whistled. The voices of other sightseers swirled around Jack and Annie. "What genius!" "The Age of Machines!" "He's the Wizard of Menlo Park!"

"Did you hear that?" Annie shouted to Jack. "Someone said something about a wizard!"

"I heard!" said Jack. *"The Wizard of Menlo Park!* We just read something about Menlo Park." He pulled out their guide book and found the page he'd been reading. He read aloud:

And of course, you will see a collection of inventions by the American grandprize winner from Menlo Park, New Jersey—Mr. Thomas Alva Edison!

"Thomas Alva Edison!" said Jack. "He's one of the most brilliant inventors who ever lived! Where's *his* exhibit?" They looked down at all the booths. Directly below them was a booth with a big sign that said EDISON.

"There! Let's go down!" said Annie.

When the moving walkway came to a staircase, Jack and Annie jumped off and hurried down to the main floor, squeezing past people as they went.

"Okay, where is it?" said Annie, looking around.

"Follow me," said Jack. He led her down a wide aisle until they came to the Edison exhibit. Lots of people were gathered around the booth.

Jack and Annie slipped through the crowd to get a good look. Many of Thomas Edison's inventions were on display. One of them had a big tube and lots of switches. Above it was a sign:

Phonograph

"What's a *phonograph*?" Annie asked.

"I think it's like an old-fashioned CD player," said Jack. "It was the first thing that played recordings of music."

A man with earphones was listening to the

phonograph. Tears ran down his wrinkled face. "It's incredible!" he said to the woman beside him. "Now we can hear the dead sing!"

"What does he mean?" Annie asked Jack.

"I guess he means that even after people die, you'll still be able to hear their voices on the recordings," said Jack.

"I never thought of it like that," said Annie.

"Shh!" someone said. People were trying to listen to a man delivering a speech to the crowd. His name tag said: HENRI.

"Yes, indeed," Henri was saying. "Thomas Alva Edison of Menlo Park, New Jersey, U.S.A., invented the phonograph, shown to the public for the first time here at the Paris World's Fair. Mr. Edison has invented many other things, too." Henri moved to another display in the booth: a lightbulb with a switch. He clicked the switch, turning the bulb on and off.

"Ten years ago, after years of work and thousands of experiments, Thomas Alva Edison invented the incandescent lightbulb," said Henri.

"When electricity passes through the thread, it gets very hot. There is no oxygen in the glass bulb, however. So the fire glows, but it does not burn."

As others moved closer to the lightbulb to get a good look, Jack turned to Annie. *"His fires glow, but they do not burn!"* he whispered. "Thomas Edison is the Magician of Light!"

"I know!" said Annie. She turned to Henri. "Excuse me—is Mr. Edison in Menlo Park now?" she asked.

"No, as a matter of fact, Mr. Edison was here at this exhibit just a short while ago," said Henri.

"Do you know where he is now?" asked Jack.

"No. All I know is that he was invited to a party and he left," said Henri.

Jack felt the hair on his neck go up. "The sorcerer," he whispered.

"Did a strange messenger in a cloak deliver the invitation?" asked Annie.

"Why, yes," said Henri.

"Do you know where the messenger went after he left here?" Jack asked.

"He asked for directions to the Pasteur Institute. That is all I know," said Henri.

"The Pasteur Institute?" said Jack. "Where's that?"

But Henri didn't answer. Another boy had asked him a question about the lightbulb.

"Come on," Annie said to Jack. "We'll find it somehow!"

As Jack and Annie left the Edison exhibit, they could hear Henri repeating his speech word for word: "Ten years ago, after years of work and thousands of experiments, Thomas Alva Edison invented the incandescent lightbulb. . . ."

CHAPTER FIVE

Hellooo?

Jack and Annie pressed through the crowd of people swarming about the Hall of Machines. Finally they reached the exit and slipped back out into the warm Paris night. The fair was just as crowded outside the hall as inside. Musicians played guitars, singers sang, food sellers shouted, "Chocolate milk! Cheese! Bread! Wine!"

"We have to get to the Pasteur Institute fast!" Annie shouted to Jack.

Jack pulled out their guide book and scanned

the index, looking for the Pasteur Institute. "It's not in here," he said. He closed the guide book. "It must not be part of the fair."

"Maybe one of those horse-and-buggies can take us there," said Annie. She pointed to a row of carriages along a street. There was a line of people waiting to get into them.

"Come on!" said Jack.

Annie and Jack made their way through the crowd and stood in the carriage line.

"Thomas Alva Edison and Alexander Graham Bell!" said Jack. "The sorcerer must think they're new magicians with secret powers!"

"And now he's invited them to some kind of party," said Annie, "so he can steal their secrets."

"I'll bet he's inviting the other two," said Jack, "the Magician of Iron and the Magician of the Invisible."

"I wonder if they're inventors, too," said Annie.

"Come on, it's our turn," said Jack.

They had reached the front of the carriage line. "We need to go to a place called the Pasteur Institute," Jack called to the coachman. "Can you take us?"

"But of course," said the man.

"Thanks!" said Annie. She and Jack climbed into the back of the open carriage. The coachman shook the reins, and his white horse clopped down the cobblestone street.

"Excuse me," Annie said, leaning forward. "But what exactly *is* the Pasteur Institute?"

"It is a laboratory for finding the cures for diseases," said the coachman.

"Oh . . . ," said Annie. "Interesting." She turned back to Jack. "Why would an evil sorcerer look for magicians in a place like that?"

"I don't know," said Jack.

"Maybe the sorcerer got sick," said Annie.

"I don't think so," said Jack. "But now we *really* need a plan. What if we run into him at the institute? Remember, he has magic powers."

"But *we* have magic powers, too," said Annie.

"Right," breathed Jack. He reached into his satchel and pulled out their book:

10 MAGIC RHYMES FOR ANNIE AND JACK FROM TEDDY AND KATHLEEN

By the light of the carriage lantern, Jack and Annie looked at the table of contents.

"Remember, we can only use a rhyme once," Jack said to Annie. *"Make a Stone Come Alive—*we've done that. *Make Helpers Appear out of Nowhere—*done that. *Mend What Cannot Be Mended—*done that."

"But we haven't used *Spin into the Air*," said Annie, "or *Make Something Disappear*, or *Find a Treasure You Must Never Lose*, or *Pull a Cloud from the Sky*, or *Turn into Ducks*."

"Go back, go back," said Jack. *"Make Something Disappear.* What about that?"

"Is a person a 'something'?" asked Annie.

"Why not?" said Jack. "This one rhyme could solve our whole problem. We'll just make the sorcerer disappear."

"Yes," breathed Annie.

"Okay, here's the plan," said Jack. "Let's memorize the rhyme now. Then as soon as we see the sorcerer, we can say it without having to look in the book."

"Great," said Annie.

Jack turned to a page in the rhyme book. "I'll memorize the line that Teddy wrote. You memorize the line in Kathleen's language," he said.

"Got it," said Annie. She looked at the rhyme and started to say her line, *"Thee-be-wan—"*

"No, don't!" yelped Jack, putting his hand over her mouth. "Don't say it out loud until we need it! You might accidentally make one of us or something really important disappear!"

"Sorry," said Annie.

"We'll practice silently," said Jack. "And we'll each only learn our own line. So neither of us can say the whole rhyme at the wrong time."

"Good plan," said Annie.

Annie studied her line silently while Jack studied his. As Jack repeated his line in his head, the carriage rolled down a busy street. The street was filled with more carriages and many bicycles. Some of the bikes were built for two people. Couples dressed in fancy evening clothes pedaled together.

Other Parisians ate by candlelight in outdoor cafés. Waiters in white aprons carried trays high in the air. Everyone seemed relaxed and cheerful. As the carriage turned onto a quiet tree-lined street, Jack wished that he and Annie could just have fun in Paris like everyone else and not be worrying about an evil sorcerer.

"Here we are!" said the driver, interrupting Jack's thoughts. He brought the carriage to a stop. "The Pasteur Institute."

"This is it?" said Jack. The Pasteur Institute

looked like a spooky mansion. Its huge front doors were closed. Its tall windows were dark.

"Are you sure we've come to the right place?" Annie asked in a small voice.

"But of course I am sure," said the coachman. "The institute appears to be closed. Would you like me to take you somewhere else?"

"No thanks," said Jack. "We'll get out here."

Annie gave the coachman a few coins. Then she and Jack climbed out of the carriage.

"Thanks," said Annie.

The coachman flicked his reins, and the white horse trotted away down the street.

Jack and Annie stared at the dark, silent building.

"I guess we should go up and knock," said Annie. She and Jack climbed the stone steps to the gigantic front doors.

"We've come to the right place," said Jack. A gas lamp lit a small metal sign that said:

Louis Pasteur Institute

Jack knocked on the door three times.

No one answered.

Annie turned the huge handle and pushed. The door was locked.

"Maybe there's another door somewhere," said Annie.

Jack and Annie walked around the institute. They knocked at a back door and a side door, but no one answered.

When they got back to the front of the building, Jack heaved a sigh. "It's no use," he said. "We've come to a complete dead end."

"We can't give up," said Annie.

"I know," said Jack. They both stood looking at the street. All was quiet, except for a few bikes rattling by.

Suddenly a whispery voice came from behind them. *"Hellooo?"*

CHAPTER SIX

Invisible Enemies

Jack and Annie whirled around. A dark figure was standing at a side door of the institute. *The sorcerer!* Jack thought. He frantically tried to remember his line of the rhyme.

"Can I help you?" the figure said. He stepped forward into the light of a gas lamp. He was an old man with stooped shoulders. His hair was white and he had a friendly smile.

"Hi! Who are you?" asked Annie.

"I am the night watchman," the man said. "The institute is closed for the night. Have you been bitten by a dog? Have you come for the rabies treatment?"

"No, we're fine," said Annie.

"Is that what you do here?" asked Jack. "You treat people for rabies?"

"Yes. Not I, of course, but Dr. Pasteur. He treats other diseases as well," said the old man. "He is the world's foremost medical researcher."

"Really?" said Jack. "What does he research?"

"Microbes," said the night watchman.

"Microbes?" said Annie.

"Germs," explained Jack.

"Yuck," said Annie.

"Microbes are invisible to the eye," said the old man. "Some are useful and necessary, but others can cause great harm. Dr. Pasteur battles the deadly ones with research and vaccines and new medicines."

Annie gasped. *"He battles deadly enemies no one can see!"* she said. "He's the Magician of the Invisible!"

"Yes!" said Jack.

The old man smiled. "I suppose you could say that," he said. "Dr. Pasteur has certainly helped a lot of people."

"We have to find him," said Annie. "Do you know where he is now?"

"Unfortunately, you have just missed him," said the night watchman. "Earlier, a messenger left an invitation for him."

"A strange man in a black cloak?" said Annie.

"You know him?" said the night watchman.

"Not really," said Jack. "But we think we know who he is. What did the invitation say?"

"I do not know," said the old man. "But when Dr. Pasteur read it, he left immediately. He said he had to get to the Eiffel Tower by ten p.m."

"The Eiffel Tower?" said Annie.

"By ten p.m.?" said Jack. "Do you know what time it is now?"

The old man pulled out a pocket watch. "It is about twenty-five minutes until ten."

"Yikes, we'd better get going!" said Annie.

"Thanks for your help," Jack said to the night watchman.

"You're welcome," the old man said. Then he stepped back inside the institute and closed the door.

"Hurry!" said Annie. She and Jack ran down the steps to the street.

"Dr. Louis Pasteur!" said Jack. "I've heard of him, too! This is crazy. None of these guys are really magicians. They're all famous for doing great things in science and stuff!"

"I wonder who the *fourth* 'magician' is," said Annie. "The Magician of Iron, who bends the metals of earth and triumphs over the wind. Is he a magician or a scientist or what?"

"I don't know," said Jack. "But we have to get to that tower fast! We have to find the magicians and learn their secrets—before the sorcerer finds them!"

Jack and Annie looked up and down the

lamp-lit street. A man was pushing a cart over the cobblestones. A couple on a two-seater bicycle rode by and disappeared. Then a horse and carriage clattered up the street.

"Taxi!" yelled Jack.

But the horse and carriage kept going. There was no sign of another one. The street was empty, except for Jack and Annie.

"Let's start walking," said Jack.

"Look," said Annie.

The couple on the two-seater bicycle rattled back down the road. They stopped near a yellow streetlamp.

"We heard you call for help. Do you need assistance?" the man asked in a gruff voice.

Jack and Annie stepped closer to the bike. The riders were an odd-looking couple. The man was short. He wore a tall black hat and had a bushy beard and a long mustache. The woman was short, also. She wore a hat with a veil that hid most of her face.

"We need to know the quickest way to the Eiffel Tower," said Annie. "We have to get there by ten. It's an emergency!"

"An emergency! Oh, dear!" exclaimed the woman in a high, squeaky voice.

The man cleared his throat and spoke in his low, gruff voice. "It would take quite a long time to walk to the Eiffel Tower from here," he said. "Perhaps you should take our bicycle."

"Really?" said Jack.

"Of course," said the man, "if it's *truly* an emergency."

"It's an emergency, all right," said Annie. "But how can we get your bike back to you?"

"Just leave it for us under the arches at the bottom of the tower," said the man.

"We can pay you for letting us borrow it," said Annie. She pulled coins out of her pocket and held them out to the couple. "You can have them all."

"No, please, we are happy to help," said the man as the couple climbed off their bicycle.

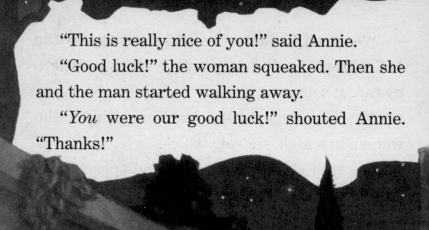

"This is really nice of you!" said Annie.

"Good luck!" the woman squeaked. Then she and the man started walking away.

"*You* were our good luck!" shouted Annie. "Thanks!"

"Yes, thanks a lot!" shouted Jack.

The man turned back. "You had better hurry!" he called over his shoulder. "If you want to be there by ten, you will have to spin like a whirlwind!" Then he and the woman rounded the corner and were gone.

"I love this bike!" said Annie. She climbed onto the front seat, and Jack climbed onto the one in back. "Ready?"

"Go easy till we get the hang of it," said Jack.

Jack and Annie started pedaling. At first, the large bike was very wobbly and they almost fell over. "We have to pedal at the same speed," said Jack.

Jack and Annie balanced themselves on the bike and tried to pedal together. The bike bumped over the cobblestones a little more smoothly.

"I think I've got the hang of it now!" said Annie.

"Me too!" said Jack. "It isn't that different from riding a regular bike."

"Which way do we go?" said Annie.

"We have to find that busy street with the cafés," said Jack.

They rode the bike to the corner and looked right and left. "That way," said Annie. She pointed to the right, where there was a busy block with lots of gaslit restaurants and people strolling about.

"Okay, go," said Jack.

Annie turned the front handlebars, and she and Jack pedaled down the bumpy street. Annie steered them carefully around couples walking arm in arm. People at outdoor cafés waved at them as they rode by.

But the street grew more deserted as Jack and Annie kept riding. By the time they came to the end, there was no one around. They pushed back on their pedals and brought their bike to a shaky stop.

"Which way now?" said Annie.

Jack looked to the right and left. Both ways were dimly lit, with closed shops and dark houses. Jack didn't recognize anything. "I don't know," he said. "I wasn't paying attention during the carriage ride."

"Me, either," said Annie.

Jack could see the Eiffel Tower rising into the sky behind other buildings. It didn't look that far away, but he had no idea how to get there. "Let's try going left," he said.

Jack and Annie turned left and rattled over the cobblestones until they came to an empty square at the end of the street.

"It's a dead end," said Jack.

"We have to go back!" said Annie. "Hurry!"

Jack and Annie turned the bike around and sped back up the street. They pedaled until they came to another dead end.

"Oh, no!" said Jack. "Where's that busy street with all the cafés?"

"We must have missed it somehow," said Annie. "We're *completely* lost! And it's almost ten o'clock!"

"This is so annoying!" said Jack. "The tower

is *right there*!" He pointed to the Eiffel Tower looming over Paris. "It's really not that far away! We just don't know how to get there!"

"Wait a minute," said Annie. "That guy said that to get there by ten, we'd have to 'spin like a whirlwind.'"

"I know, but we're lost!" said Jack. "We don't know which way to go!"

"It doesn't matter!" said Annie. "We have to spin! *Spin into the Air!* That's one of our magic rhymes! *We have to spin our bike into the air!*"

CHAPTER SEVEN

Start Pedaling!

"**W**ow," whispered Jack. He reached into his satchel and pulled out their rhyme book.

"I'll say the first line of the rhyme," Jack said to Annie. "You say the second. Then we'll start pedaling as fast as we can. The street's empty. No one will see us. So we can—"

"Good," interrupted Annie. "Let's get going."

Jack held up the rhyme book so they could both read by the light of a streetlamp. He read his line first:

Whirl and twirl and swirl and spin!

Then Annie read the second line:

Tee-roll-eye-bee-eye-ben!

Jack shoved the book back into his satchel. "Pedal!" he cried.

Jack and Annie balanced themselves on the bike and pedaled hard. The bike rattled over the cobblestones.

"Faster!" shouted Jack. He pedaled as hard as he could.

The bike shot forward! The front wheel began rising off the stone pavement!

"Whoa!" cried Annie.

"Hold on tight!" cried Jack.

Jack gripped his handlebars as the wheels spun faster and faster and the bicycle rose into the air. It rose higher and higher above the dark street, above the rooftops, and into the moon-bright sky.

"Turn left!" shouted Jack.

Annie turned her handlebars, and the flying bicycle headed straight toward the Eiffel Tower.

The white beams of the tower's spotlights swept over Paris, shining on chimneys, church steeples, and domes. But Jack kept his eyes fixed on the glowing iron tower. That was where they had to go. That was their goal.

As Jack and Annie pedaled, the warm Paris air embraced them, holding the bike steady. With very little effort, they drew closer and closer to the tower. Soon they were almost there.

"We have to land!" shouted Jack.

"I know!" shouted Annie. "Lean forward!"

They both leaned forward. The front wheel of the bike dipped. Annie steadied her handlebars as the bike zoomed down toward the base of the tower.

"Stop pedaling!" shouted Jack. He was afraid they would dive straight into the ground.

But the bike seemed to have a mind of its own. As it drew nearer to the base of the tower, it began to drop softly and slowly, like a falling feather.

The bike floated closer and closer to the

ground. Its wheels brushed the grass of a shadowy garden not far from the tower. Jack and Annie pushed on the brakes and the bike slowed to a stop. Then it fell gently onto its side, dumping Jack and Annie onto the soft, wet grass.

Jack looked up. The Eiffel Tower loomed above them, reaching toward the bright Paris moon.

"We made it," Annie said breathlessly.

"Not yet," said Jack. "We still have to find that party." He and Annie stood up.

"But first we have to leave the bike under the tower, like we promised," said Annie.

Jack and Annie picked up the big bike. They jumped back on and started pedaling toward the Eiffel Tower. The bike felt a lot clunkier on the ground than it had in the air. As they bumped over the grass, they saw people streaming away from the fairgrounds.

"It looks like the fair's closing," said Annie.

Jack and Annie parked the bike in a bike stand beneath the tower. The area looked deserted. There was no sign of a party or of the new magicians. A single guard stood under one of the tall arches.

"Excuse me!" Annie called to the guard. "Do you know what time it is?"

"Almost ten," answered the guard.

"Is the tower closed for the day?" said Jack.

"Yes, I'm afraid it is," said the guard.

"We heard there was going to be a party at the Eiffel Tower tonight," said Annie.

The guard shook his head. "No, sorry. As you can see, there is no party here—unless you mean the private affair at the top of the tower."

"There's a private party at the very top?" said Annie. She and Jack looked up. The top of the tower seemed a mile away.

"Yes, with some very important guests," said the guard. He leaned closer and whispered, "Mr. Thomas Edison, Dr. Louis Pasteur, and Mr. Alexander Graham Bell."

"That's our party!" exclaimed Annie.

"Is there a fourth guest?" Jack asked.

"There may be others, but I did not see anyone else go up," said the guard.

"We need to be there, too," said Annie. "How do we get up?"

The guard smiled. "I am sorry," he said, "but the elevators are all shut down for the night. Even if you had an invitation, the only way you could get to the top would be to climb the steps." The guard looked up. "And that is quite a few steps, indeed. Come back bright and early tomorrow and you can ride the elevators." The guard tipped his hat and strolled away.

"Excuse me, sir!" Annie called after him. "Just how many steps are there?"

"To be exact, there are 1,652 steps to the platform at the top of the Eiffel Tower," the guard said. Then he disappeared into the dark.

"That's too many steps," said Jack.

"Let's fly up on the bike!" said Annie.

"We can't," said Jack. "We can only use a rhyme once, remember?" He pulled out their book of rhymes and read the ones they hadn't used. *"Find a Treasure You Must Never Lose."*

"That doesn't help," said Annie.

"Pull a Cloud from the Sky," read Jack.

"No help there, either," said Annie.

"Turn into Ducks," read Jack.

Annie smiled.

"Forget it. I'm not meeting Thomas Edison as a duck," said Jack.

"So . . . ?" said Annie.

"The steps," said Jack.

Jack and Annie moved quickly around the base of the tower, searching for steps. "There!" said Jack. They hurried to a staircase tucked inside one of the legs of the tower.

Jack gripped the iron railing. "Ready?" he said.

"Yep," said Annie. "Let's go."

Together they started up the 1,652 steps that led to the top platform of the Eiffel Tower.

CHAPTER EIGHT

Secrets

Jack could see the Paris sky through the iron rails of the tower. At first, climbing was easy. The steps weren't very steep, and Jack counted each one as they climbed. "Twenty-six, twenty-seven, twenty-eight . . ."

"I wonder what's going on at the top now," said Annie.

"Thirty-one, thirty-two, thirty-three," breathed Jack.

"I wonder if the sorcerer is there with the others," said Annie. "What will he do when he

finds out those guys aren't the kind of magicians
he thinks they are?"

"Don't know," breathed Jack. "Forty-nine,
fifty."

"I'll bet he won't believe them!" said Annie.
"He might kidnap them—and *force* them to tell
their secrets."

"Sixty-one, sixty-two . . . ," said Jack.

"Faster, faster," said Annie.

By the time Jack had counted the 360 steps to the tower's first-story platform, they were both panting. Jack's feet felt like lead.

"That's a lot of steps!" said Annie, out of breath.

"No . . . no kidding," said Jack, gasping between words. "But we . . . we have to keep going!"

They kept going—but a little more slowly. Jack picked up the count: "Three hundred sixty-one . . . three hundred sixty-two . . ."

"You can see how he might have thought Alexander Graham Bell was a new magician," said Annie, panting.

"Three hundred ninety-two . . . three hundred ninety-three . . . ," said Jack.

"Think about it!" said Annie. "You've never used a phone in your life . . . then one day you pick up this thing . . . hear a voice talking . . . the voice of someone . . . who lives far away . . . you'd think . . ."

"Magic!" breathed Jack. "Four hundred forty-four . . . four hundred forty-five . . ."

"And Thomas Edison!" said Annie. "Think about it! Thousands of years . . . you depend on fire for light . . . then one day . . . you flip a switch . . . *presto!* . . . a glass bulb lights up. . . ."

"Magic!" gasped Jack. "Five hundred ten . . . five hundred eleven . . ."

"And Louis Pasteur . . . think about it!" said Annie. "There are all these diseases . . . nobody knows what's causing them . . . then one day . . . this guy discovers germs . . . and he figures out a way . . . to wipe out the bad ones!"

"Magic!" said Jack. "Six hundred two . . . six hundred three . . . six hundred four . . ."

"I can't believe the sorcerer would do anything mean to these guys!" said Annie. "Even if he is . . ."

"Evil . . . ," said Jack. "Six hundred twenty . . . six hundred twenty-one . . ." His leg muscles burned, but he moved like a machine up the mountain of steps. Finally they reached the second platform. "Seven hundred!" breathed Jack.

"We have . . . to keep going," said Annie.

"Keep going . . . and let's get . . . our rhyme ready," said Jack. "As soon as we see . . . the sorcerer . . . we have to say it . . . make him disappear!"

"Right," breathed Annie. "That's our mission! Protect . . . the new magicians . . . and find out . . . their secrets . . . for Merlin. . . ."

"Don't talk . . . save breath . . . ," said Jack.

Jack and Annie kept climbing and counting. Drawing closer to the top of the tower, Jack heard piano music. As they climbed higher, the music grew louder.

Finally, Jack and Annie climbed onto a third platform. "One thousand six hundred and fifty-two!" gasped Jack. They were almost at the very top of the tower. A spiral staircase led from the platform up to a terrace.

Jack's leg muscles ached, his head hurt,

his heart pounded. "But we have to keep . . .
going . . . ," he whispered. He and Annie dragged
themselves up the spiral staircase that led to the
terrace.

They both collapsed and sat on the top step,
trying to breathe. A flag overhead flapped noisily.
Damp with sweat, Jack felt chilled by the wind.

The piano music was coming from a small
apartment on the terrace.

"I wonder who's . . . playing," said Annie, still
gasping for breath.

"Maybe one of the . . . magicians," said Jack.

"Or the . . . the sorcerer," said Annie.

Jack felt a surge of fear. It almost took away
his tiredness. "We have to . . . make him disappear," he said. He stood up shakily.

"Let's look through the window," said Annie.

The two of them struggled against the wind
as they staggered to the window of the apartment. When they peeked in, they saw a cozy
room with leather chairs and glowing lamps. A

man with a trim, pointed beard was playing the piano. Behind him stood an elderly man with a graying beard, a big man with a bushy white beard, and a friendly-looking man with no beard.

All of them were smiling and nodding their heads in time to the music.

"There're four of them in there," whispered Jack.

"Is the fourth one the sorcerer?" said Annie. "Or is he the fourth new magician?"

"I don't think any of them are the sorcerer," whispered Jack. "None of them look evil. They all look pretty nice."

"What is this place, anyway?" said Annie.

"Let's check the book," said Jack. He pulled out the guide book and looked up *Eiffel Tower*. He found a drawing of the tower. Each platform was labeled. The area at the top read:

At the very top of the tower is the apartment of Gustave Eiffel.

A picture showed Gustave Eiffel sitting in his apartment.

"Look, he's the guy playing the piano!" said Jack. He read on:

Gustave Eiffel is one of the world's master engineers. He built the Eiffel Tower with glass and iron, the world's newest building materials. Since these materials are lighter than stone or brick, structures can be built very tall.

The tower's open design and its iron beams keep it stable in strong winds.

"He's the fourth magician!" whispered Jack. "The Magician of Iron—*he bends the metals of earth and triumphs over the wind!*"

"They're all together now," said Annie. "Alexander Graham Bell, Thomas Edison, Louis Pasteur, and Gustave Eiffel—the four new magicians."

"And the evil sorcerer hasn't shown up yet," said Jack.

"Come on," said Annie. "We have to warn them about him!"

"And find out their secrets before *he* does!" said Jack. He and Annie walked to the door of the apartment. Annie knocked.

The night fell silent as the piano music stopped.

Oh, brother, thought Jack. How would they explain such a weird situation to these famous men?

The door of the apartment opened. Gustave Eiffel looked out. "Yes?" he said.

"Hello. Can we come in?" asked Annie.

Mr. Eiffel looked startled. "Goodness, I seem to be having many unexpected guests tonight. How did you get up here, little girl? I thought the elevators were closed."

"My brother and I climbed the stairs," said Annie.

"Oh, my! That's a very long climb for two children!" said Mr. Eiffel. "Or anyone else, for that matter! Did someone invite you to a party here, too?"

"Not exactly," said Annie.

"Well, come in anyway. The more the merrier!" Mr. Eiffel stepped back to let Annie and Jack inside. Then he closed the door behind them.

The four men looked curiously at Jack and Annie.

"Before you tell us about yourselves, allow me to introduce my other unexpected guests," said Mr. Eiffel. "This is Dr. Louis Pasteur." He pointed to the elderly man with the graying beard. "And Mr. Alexander Graham Bell." The big man with the white beard nodded. "And Mr. Thomas Alva Edison."

The friendly-looking man reached out and shook both of their hands, first Annie's, then Jack's. "You can call me Alva," Mr. Edison said.

"Hi, Alva," Jack murmured shyly. He couldn't believe he was shaking hands with Thomas Alva Edison.

"You can call us Jack and Annie," said Annie.

"So, Jack and Annie, how did you learn about this gathering?" Mr. Eiffel asked. "You have nothing to do with the invitations these gentlemen received, do you?"

"We . . . um . . ." Annie smiled a goofy grin, as if she didn't know what to say next. She took a deep breath. "Well, no," she said. "But we know who sent them."

"Who?" asked Mr. Eiffel.

"An evil sorcerer who wants to steal the secrets of your magic," said Annie.

"An evil sorcerer?" said Mr. Eiffel.

"Yes," said Annie. "We can make him disappear, but we need you to tell us your secrets before he gets here."

The four men just stared at her.

"What did she say?" asked Mr. Edison, as if he were a little hard of hearing.

"She says an evil sorcerer wants to steal the secrets of our magic," Mr. Eiffel said loudly. "And that we must tell them our secrets before the sorcerer arrives."

Mr. Edison laughed. So did the others.

Jack felt his face grow red.

"The secrets of our magic, eh?" said Mr. Eiffel. "That's really a very good question. Let's think. ... I believe the secret of *my* magic is actually quite simple. I have a taste for adventure and a love of work and responsibility. So the challenge of building the tallest structure in the world was greatly appealing to me."

"Very good," said Annie. "Taste for adventure, love of work and responsibility." She turned to Dr. Pasteur. "Doctor, what's your secret?"

"My secret?" said Dr. Pasteur. He looked down at the floor for a long moment. Then he looked up and said, "I believe my secret is this: Chance favors the prepared mind."

The other men nodded.

"Hmm," said Mr. Bell.

"Ah," said Mr. Eiffel.

"Indeed," said Mr. Edison.

"Um . . . what does that mean?" said Annie.

"*Chance* means *luck*," explained Dr. Pasteur. "I daresay we all hope for a bit of luck in our work. But I find the more I study and prepare, the luckier I become."

"Oh, that makes good sense," said Annie. "Studying makes you luckier." She turned to Mr. Edison. "Alva, what's your secret?"

Mr. Edison smiled modestly. "Well, let me see." His eyes were bright and twinkling. "I suppose my secret is this: Genius is one percent inspiration and ninety-nine percent perspiration."

The other men laughed.

"That's right," said Mr. Eiffel. "Sweat! Hard work! Thousands of experiments fail—then finally one works!"

The other men clapped.

"I get it!" said Annie. "Genius is mostly sweat."

Everyone then turned to the last magician.

"Oh, my," said Mr. Bell. He stroked his bushy white beard. "How shall I say it?" He closed his eyes. "When one door closes, another door opens."

Everyone started to applaud.

"Wait, there's more!" Keeping his eyes closed, Mr. Bell continued. "We often look so long and so regretfully upon the closed door that we do not see the new ones which open for us." He looked at everyone and smiled. The other men clapped again.

"Yes, yes!" said Mr. Eiffel. "There's always another door."

"Never give up hope!" said Annie. "Got it!"

Mr. Eiffel smiled at Annie. "So, do you think our secrets would satisfy your evil sorcerer?"

Before Annie could answer, there was a loud knocking on the door.

CHAPTER NINE

The Sorcerer

Jack's knees turned to jelly.

The knocking came again.

Mr. Eiffel laughed. "Goodness, *another* unexpected guest!" He started toward the door.

"Don't open it!" Jack shouted.

Everyone looked at Jack as if he were crazy.

"It's the sorcerer!" Jack said. "My sister was telling the truth! He thinks you're all magicians!"

"Don't be afraid, son," Dr. Pasteur said to Jack. "I'm sure it's just another guest."

Mr. Eiffel stepped toward the door.

"No, please!" shouted Jack.

Mr. Eiffel opened the door. There was a deafening clap of thunder! A ball of fire blasted into the room!

Jack covered his face.

Then all was quiet.

"Jack?" Annie said in a small voice.

Jack looked up. A golden haze had filled the room. Annie stepped quickly to Jack's side. But none of the others moved. Mr. Eiffel, Mr. Bell, Mr. Edison, and Dr. Pasteur were all as still as stone.

Jack could barely make out a dark figure in a long cloak standing in the doorway.

"It's him!" Jack cried. "We have to say our rhyme!" Jack shouted the line he had memorized:

Thing before us, now we see—

Jack waited for Annie to finish the rhyme. But she didn't say her line. *Oh, no! She's forgotten it!* Jack thought wildly.

Suddenly he heard Annie laugh. "It's *you*," she said.

Jack looked up. The haze had cleared. The sorcerer's face glowed in the light. It was a familiar face, craggy with electric-blue eyes.

"Merlin?" breathed Jack.

The master magician answered him with a smile.

"Merlin! Hi!" said Annie. She rushed over and hugged him.

Jack just stared at Merlin. "What happened?" he asked. "Where's the evil sorcerer?"

"There *are* evil sorcerers in my world," Merlin said in his deep voice. "But I assure you none of them were here at the World's Fair today."

"So *you* were the messenger?" said Annie. "*You* delivered the invitations for everyone to come to the top of the tower?"

"Yes, I was the messenger," said Merlin. "I wanted to gather these remarkable men together so you could meet them all in the short time you had to spend in Paris."

"But why did you tell us that we had to find them before an evil sorcerer did?" said Jack.

Merlin smiled. "Without that challenge, would you have used all your powers of thinking and courage?" he asked. "Would you have been so determined to find the 'new magicians' and learn their secrets?"

"Well, maybe not," Jack said honestly.

"Problems make us focus our energy," said Merlin. "They can help us think more sharply and act more swiftly. Never wish for all your problems to disappear. Problems can help you achieve your goals. Do you understand?"

Jack and Annie nodded.

"So now, what *are* the secrets of these remarkable men?" asked Merlin. "I truly wish to know."

"If you want to reach your goal, you have to love adventure and responsibility," said Jack.

"You have to study and be prepared so luck will favor you," said Annie.

"You have to work really hard, because

genius is ninety-nine percent perspiration and only one percent inspiration," said Jack.

"And you should never lose hope," said Annie, "because when one door closes, another one opens, and you don't want to miss it."

"Wonderful!" said Merlin. "These are excellent secrets! And I believe you not only *learned* them on this mission, but you *lived* each of them as well. Do you understand?"

"I guess," said Jack.

Annie looked at the four frozen men. "What about *them*, Merlin?" she said anxiously. "Will they be okay?"

"Yes, they will awaken as soon as I leave. Do not worry," said Merlin.

"I'm sorry I almost made you disappear," said Jack.

Merlin smiled. "That is quite all right. But now we have a little problem. One must never leave a magic rhyme hanging in the air unfinished."

"Oh," said Jack. "So Annie needs to finish the rhyme and make something disappear?"

"Precisely," said Merlin. "Perhaps you could use the rhyme to speed me back to Camelot."

"Sure," said Annie. "But do you have to leave so soon?"

"Yes, I must be on my way," said Merlin. "I would not want to confuse these kind gentlemen. Do not worry. I will send for you both again in the very near future. But now it is time for me to . . . disappear."

Jack smiled. "Good-bye, Merlin," he said.

Annie took a deep breath. Then she looked at Merlin and slowly said her line:

Thee-be-wan-new-ee-vee!

There was a clap of thunder and a blast of fiery light—and Merlin was gone.

Just as suddenly, the new magicians came back to life. Mr. Eiffel pointed to the open doorway as wind gusted inside. "You see, son," he said to Jack, "it was only the wind."

"Oh, yeah," said Jack, pretending to be embarrassed. "I'm sorry."

"Don't worry," said Mr. Eiffel. "You and your sister are perfectly safe. We live in the wondrous new world of science, and not in the old world of magic and sorcerers."

Mr. Eiffel moved toward the open doorway. "Come, let us all step outside and take a look at our new world."

Everyone joined him on the windy terrace and looked over the railing.

"Paris is a lovely city, is it not?" Mr. Eiffel said.

Jack and Annie and the others watched the giant spotlights sweep over Paris like white comets. The lights shined down on the domes and treetops, the grand monuments and church spires, the colorful fountain waters and rippling river. The boat lights twinkled like fireflies.

"Thanks to Mr. Eiffel and his tower, we can see the entire city," Mr. Edison shouted above the wind.

"Thanks to Mr. Edison, ten thousand gas streetlamps in Paris will soon be replaced by electric lights!" said Mr. Eiffel.

"Thanks to Dr. Pasteur's institute, we will soon have cures for many more deadly diseases," said Mr. Bell.

"And thanks to Mr. Bell, I'll be able to call you all on the telephone and tell you about it!" joked Dr. Pasteur.

Everyone laughed.

"And this is just the beginning!" said Annie. "Someday people will carry tiny telephones in their pockets and talk to other people anywhere in the world."

"Uh, Annie, we'd better be going," said Jack. He didn't want the others to know he and Annie were from the future.

But Annie kept talking. "And there'll be these things called computers," she said, "that can give you instant information about anything, anytime—"

"*Annie!*" said Jack.

"And get this!" she said. She pointed to the full moon overhead. "Someday people will actually walk on that moon up there!"

The men all chuckled. "You have a most delightful imagination," said Mr. Eiffel.

"And that is a wonderful thing!" said Mr. Edison. "Without imagination, none of us would be standing here tonight."

"Well, we'd better be getting home now," said Jack.

"And where *is* your home? The moon?" teased Mr. Eiffel.

"No, it's Frog Creek, Pennsylvania, in the United States," said Jack.

"How will you get there?" said Mr. Bell.

"In our magic tree house," said Annie.

The men laughed. Jack tried to laugh with them. "Ha. Good one, Annie," he said. "Well, let's go."

"Annie, I hope you and your brother have a safe trip in your magic tree house," said Mr.

Eiffel. "You have both been most entertaining guests. Please come visit me anytime."

Jack and Annie waved good-bye to the four men. Then they climbed carefully down the spiral staircase and started down the 1,652 steps of the Eiffel Tower.

CHAPTER TEN

Good Night, Magicians!

It was much easier walking *down* 1,652 steps than walking up. Jack and Annie walked down and down and down and down and down and down and down and down and down and down and down—until finally they stepped onto the ground.

Jack noticed that the two-seater bicycle was gone. "I guess those two people came and got their bike," he said.

Jack and Annie looked around. Exhibits were covered and gates were locked. All the motion and noise of the World's Fair had ended for the day. The living encyclopedia had gone to sleep. Suddenly Jack felt very exhausted.

"Home?" said Annie.

Jack nodded. "Frog Creek," he said, sighing.

Jack and Annie hurried over the bridge and across the avenue. "Those guys were really nice," said Jack as they walked through the dark, rose-scented park.

"I know," said Annie. "They acted like regular people. But they've done all those amazing things."

"Yeah," said Jack. "They're like magicians in disguise."

Jack and Annie came to the magic tree house. They climbed up the rope ladder and looked one last time out the window. The Eiffel Tower seemed to stand watch over Paris, its spotlights sweeping over the city.

Jack pulled Merlin's letter out of his satchel. He opened it and pointed to the words *Frog Creek*. "I wish we could go—"

Before Jack could finish making the wish, he and Annie were bathed in brilliant white light. Jack looked up. One of the beams of the tower's spotlights had come to rest on the tree house. It shined on them for a long moment.

With both hands, Annie waved wildly into the blinding light. Jack waved, too.

"Good night, magicians!" Annie shouted.

Jack laughed. Then he pointed at Merlin's

letter again and finished his wish: ". . . home to Frog Creek," he said.

The wind started to blow.

The tree house started to spin.

It spun faster and faster.

Then everything was still.

Absolutely still.

Jack opened his eyes. He and Annie were dressed in their regular clothes again. Dusky light filtered into the tree house. No time at all had passed in Frog Creek.

"That was a great trip," Jack said softly.

"Really great," said Annie.

Jack pulled the guide book to the 1889 Paris World's Fair out of his backpack. He left it on the tree house floor along with Merlin's letter. But he kept Teddy and Kathleen's book of magic rhymes.

"So. We have three rhymes left for our fourth adventure," he said.

"Quack, quack," said Annie.

"Very funny," said Jack. "Ready?"

"Yep," said Annie. She climbed down the rope ladder, and Jack followed.

As they started walking through the darkening woods, the world felt familiar and ordinary again. "I can't believe we just met all those guys," said Jack. "I can't believe I actually shook hands with Thomas Edison."

"You mean with Alva," said Annie.

"Yeah. Alva. . . .Wow," Jack said softly.

"What do you think Merlin meant when he said that we had *lived* all their secrets, as well as *learned* them?" said Annie.

"Well, think about it," said Jack. "We wouldn't have gone on our mission in the first place if we didn't have a love for adventure and responsibility—like Mr. Eiffel."

"Right," said Annie. "And we sure put a lot of sweat into our mission—when we climbed the stairs."

"And we didn't lose hope when the door of the institute was locked," said Jack. "We stuck around until another door opened."

"And you prepared us by reading from the research book," said Annie, "so chance favored us when we heard someone call Thomas Edison 'the Wizard of Menlo Park.'"

"And chance favored us when those two people lent us their bike," said Jack.

"Actually, I don't think that was chance," Annie said.

"What do you mean?" said Jack.

"Did you notice that man looked more like a kid in disguise?" said Annie. "His beard and mustache looked kind of fakey."

"I *did* notice that!" said Jack. "But there was so much going on, I didn't have time to think about it."

"And the woman talked in that funny, squeaky voice, and the veil of her hat covered her face," said Annie. "And the guy told us to spin like a whirlwind. That was a weird thing to say, but it reminded us of the rhyme in Teddy and Kathleen's book."

Jack nodded slowly. Then he smiled. "You think those two were actually Teddy and Kathleen?" he said.

"Maybe," said Annie. "On our last three missions, I felt like they were with us, helping us get to the right place at the right time."

"Next time, maybe we can catch them when they help us," said Jack.

Annie laughed. "Yeah, we'll try to surprise *them* for a change!"

"Good plan," said Jack.

A bell jingled in the distance.

"Ice cream!" said Annie.

"Yep, that's our mission now!" said Jack.

The ice cream bell jingled again. Jack and Annie ran out of the woods into the soft summer twilight.

Author's Note

The famous words of **Alexander Graham Bell** have given many people hope in the face of disappointment: "When one door closes another door opens. But we so often look so long and so regretfully upon the closed door, that we do not see the ones which open for us."

Bell tried many doors as he attempted to invent a device that could transmit a human request. After countless experiments, while working on his invention one day, Bell called out to his assistant in the next room: "Mr. Watson, come here." To their surprise, Watson heard

Bell's request over a transmitter they'd been working on. These turned out to be the first words ever heard over a telephone.

When **Thomas Alva Edison** gave his famous quote, "Genius is one percent inspiration and ninety-nine percent perspiration," he really meant it! He was always a hard worker. As a child, Edison read nearly every book in the public library. When he was only twelve, he sold snacks on trains and had another business selling vegetables. When he was thirteen, he started his own newspaper, and at fifteen he became an expert telegraph operator.

In his spare time, Edison worked on inventions. Early on, a blow to his ear and a case of scarlet fever damaged his hearing. The silence of his deafness only helped him concentrate. Eventually Edison opened a laboratory in Menlo Park, New Jersey. There he invented the first incandescent electric lightbulb and the first phonograph, or record player. A few years later, he created the first silent motion pictures. By the end of his career, Edison had patents for over

1,000 inventions. When he died in 1931, households all over America dimmed their electric lights to honor him.

By the time **Louis Pasteur** stated that "chance favors the prepared mind," he had learned a lot about being well prepared. As a medical researcher in Paris, Pasteur studied microbes for many years. He hoped to understand how germs and infectious diseases were related. Pasteur's hard work led to the "germ theory" in medicine. He developed a life-saving vaccine to fight rabies, and he created a process called "pasteurization" that uses heat to kill germs in food. Today the Pasteur Institute in Paris is still a very important medical research center that helps prevent and treat deadly diseases.

The French engineer **Gustave Eiffel** gave much credit for his success to his parents. He said, "From my father I inherited a taste for adventure, from my mother a love of work and responsibility." Eiffel had many great adventures in his career. Using the new technology of building with iron, he designed innovative bridges and viaducts. He even helped design the Statue of Liberty for New York City. But his most amazing feat was the Eiffel Tower in Paris, the tallest structure in the world until 1930.

Eiffel faced a lot of resistance to building the tower. At first, many people thought the design was terribly ugly; others were sure the tower would topple over in strong winds. But Eiffel had designed his tower so that the wind could blow safely through its open latticework. In time it became the most beloved symbol of Paris. Today the Eiffel Tower has over 6 million visitors a year.

Thomas Alva Edison actually met with Gustave Eiffel in Eiffel's tower office during the 1889 Paris World's Fair. Also on his visit to Paris, Edison met with Louis Pasteur at the Pasteur Institute. The only one of the four great men not in Paris that summer was Alexander Graham Bell, but a display of his new telephone invention was one of the most popular exhibits at the World's Fair.

Fun Activities for Jack and Annie and *You*!

Puzzle of the New Magicians

Jack and Annie learned many new things on their adventure at the 1889 World's Fair. Did you?

Put your knowledge to the test with this puzzle. You can use a notebook or make a copy of this page if you don't want to write in your book.

1. The inventor of the lightbulb.

☐ ☐ ◯ ☐ ☐ ☐

2. The first invention to ever record and play back sound.

☐ ☐ ☐ ◯ ☐ ☐ ☐ ☐ ☐ ☐

3. A doctor whose research led to many medicines and vaccines.

☐ ☐ ◯ ☐ ☐ ☐ ☐

4. Another word for the tiny particles we call germs.

☐ ☐ ◯ ☐ ☐ ☐ ☐ ☐

5. The inventor of the telephone.

☐ ◯ ☐ ☐

6. The famous iron tower in Paris and the name of the man who designed it.

◯ ☐ ☐ ☐ ☐ ☐

7. The country where the 1889 World's Fair was held.

☐ ☐ ☐ ☐ ◯ ☐

Now look at your answers above. The letters that are circled spell a word—but that word is scrambled! Can you unscramble it to spell the kind of magic the new magicians practiced?

Be a New Magician!

Alexander Graham Bell's telephone works because of vibrations. In his phone, sound vibrations travel along an electric current. But electricity is not the only thing that will carry vibrations and make sound travel. Try this experiment with a friend or family member and see if you can conjure up a telephone out of string and a couple of plastic cups!

String Telephone

You will need:

- 2 plastic cups
- 3–10 yards of string
- sharpened pencil
- 2 paper clips (optional)

With the sharpened pencil, poke a small hole in the bottom of each cup. Thread the string through the hole of one cup. Tie a knot at the end of the string inside the cup so it can't pull through. You can also tie the string to a paper clip to be extra sure it will stay in place.

Then thread the other end of the string through the second cup from the outside. Knot the inside end or tie it to the other paper clip.

One person should hold one cup and the other person hold the other. Walk away from each other until the string is tight. One of you hold your cup up to your ear. The other should talk into the cup. Can you hear each other?

An Electric Idea!

Thomas Alva Edison used very powerful and dangerous electricity for his experiments with the lightbulb. He was an expert and knew what he was doing. **Never touch the outlets or experiment with the electricity in your home!**

There is one kind of electricity that is safe to try—static electricity. That's the electricity that can sometimes make your hair stand on end or give you a little shock when you touch someone. If you've ever wondered whether static electricity is real electricity, try this experiment.

Static Light

You will need:

- a fluorescent lightbulb (Note: this is not the kind of lightbulb Edison invented. Ask an adult to be sure you're using a fluorescent bulb.)
- a comb
- any dark room

Go into the dark room. Run the comb quickly through your dry hair over and over. Or rub it on a sweater. Then touch the comb to the lightbulb and look closely. You should see little sparks. Static electricity is strong enough to light up a lightbulb!

Here's a special preview of

Magic Tree House #36
(A Merlin Mission)
Blizzard of the Blue Moon

Jack and Annie go on another amazing
adventure filled with history, magic,
and lots of snow!

Available now!

CHAPTER ONE

The Last Unicorn

The November sky was gray with clouds. Jack sat reading in front of the living room fire.

"Who wants hot chocolate?" his dad called from the kitchen.

"Me, please!" said Jack.

The front door burst open, and with a gust of cold wind, Annie rushed inside. "Jack! Guess what!" she whispered. "It's back!"

"How do you know?" said Jack.

"I was walking home from the library"— Annie paused to catch her breath—"and I saw a flash in the sky above the woods. The last time that happened—"

Before she could finish the sentence, Jack jumped up. "Dad, Annie and I are going to go outside for a while!" he shouted. "Can the hot chocolate wait till we get back?"

"Sure, have fun!" their dad called from the kitchen.

"I have to get my pack," Jack said to Annie. "Meet you on the porch."

"Don't forget the rhyme book!" said Annie.

Annie slipped outside and Jack ran up to his room. He grabbed his backpack. He checked to make sure their book of magic rhymes was inside. *Good*, there it was.

10
Magic Rhymes
for
Annie and Jack
from
Teddy and Kathleen

Jack charged back downstairs. He pulled on his boots, put on his jacket, tied a scarf around his neck, grabbed his mittens, and headed out the door.

"Come on!" said Annie.

Jack could see his breath in the cold air. "Brrr," he said. "Let's hurry!"

Jack and Annie ran down the street and into the Frog Creek woods. They wove between the trees, their boots crunching through the fallen leaves.

Jack stopped. The magic tree house *was* back. High in a tall oak tree, it was silhouetted against the gray November sky. "You were right," he said to Annie. "Good work."

"Thanks," Annie said. She ran to the rope ladder and started up. Jack followed her.

When they climbed inside the tree house, Jack and Annie saw a book and a scroll of parchment paper lying on the floor. Annie picked up the scroll, unrolled it, and read aloud.

Dear Jack and Annie of Frog Creek,

I am sending you on one more mission to prove that you can use magic wisely. This poem will guide you.

—M.

The very last unicorn
Is now hidden well
By those who have put him
Under a spell.

Four centuries, four decades
From that afternoon,
At the end of November,
Before the blue moon,

He will wake once more
And be free to go home
If you call out his name:
Divine Flower of Rome.

You must coax him to stand
Once his name is spoken.

His chain will break
And the spell, too, be broken.

Then a young girl must love him
And show him the way,
Lest he be trapped forever
On public display.

If he loses this chance
To rise and depart,
All magic will fade
From his horn and his heart.

"A unicorn!" breathed Annie. "I love him already. *I'll* show him the way!"

"But this poem is really hard to understand," said Jack. "What kind of research book did Morgan send us?"

He picked up the book that had been left for them by Morgan le Fay, the librarian of Camelot. The cover showed a row of skyscrapers. The title was *New York City Guide Book, 1938*.

"New York City?" said Annie. "I love New

York City! Remember the great time we had there with Aunt Mallory?"

"Yeah, I love it, too," said Jack. "But why would there be a unicorn in New York City in 1938? A unicorn is an ancient fantasy creature. New York City's a real place, and 1938 is not even that long ago."

"You're right," said Annie. "It sounds like a hard mission. But don't forget we have Teddy and Kathleen's magic rhymes to help us."

"Yeah," said Jack. He pulled out the book

given to them by their friends Teddy and Kathleen, two young enchanters of Camelot. "The problem is, we can only use each rhyme once, and we've already used seven out of the ten."

"Which means we still have three left," said Annie. "What are they?"

"Pull a Cloud from the Sky," said Jack.

"Cool," said Annie.

"Yeah, it is," said Jack. "But I'm not sure it will be much use." He looked back at the book. *"Find a Treasure You Must Never Lose,"* he said.

"Hey, that's a really good one!" said Annie. "The unicorn's a treasure. So that rhyme could take care of our whole mission."

"But it only *partly* fits," said Jack. "You could call the unicorn a treasure. But once we find him, we *have* to lose him. He has to go back home."

"Oh, right . . . ," said Annie. "What else?"

"Your favorite," said Jack. *"Turn into Ducks."*

Annie laughed. "I can't wait to use that one!" she said.

"I hope we *never* use that one," said Jack. He didn't want to waddle around and quack like a duck. "These leftover rhymes don't seem very helpful to me."

"Well, let's just wait and see," said Annie. "But now . . ." She held up Morgan's research book and smiled.

Jack nodded. "New York City, here we come," he said. He pointed at the book's cover. "I wish we could go *there*!"

The wind started to blow.

The tree house started to spin.

It spun faster and faster.

Then everything was still.

Absolutely still.

Get your
Official
Magic Tree House
PASSPORT!
www.magictreehouse.com

AROUND THE WORLD WITH JACK AND ANNIE

Around the World with Jack and Annie!

You have traveled to far away places and have been
on countless Magic Tree House adventures.
Now is your chance to receive an official
Magic Tree House passport and collect official stamps
for each destination from around the world!

HOW

Get your exclusive Magic Tree House Passport!*

Send your name, street address, city, state, zip code, and date of birth to:
The Magic Tree House Passport, Random House Children's Books,
Marketing Department, 1745 Broadway, 10th Floor, New York, NY 10019

OR log on to **www.magictreehouse.com**
to download and print your passport now!

Collect Official Magic Tree House Stickers:

Log on to **www.magictreehouse.com** to submit your answer to the
trivia questions below. If you answer correctly, you will automatically
receive your official sticker for Book 35: *Night of the New Magicians*.

1. Who invented the telephone?

2. What city in New Jersey is Thomas Edison from?

3. What borrowed object do Jack and Annie "spin into the air"?

*One passport per person. No purchase necessary. While supplies last. Allow 6 to 8 weeks for delivery. Passports available beginning March 2007.

Read all the Magic Tree House adventures for a chance to collect them all! RHCB

Discover the facts
behind the fiction with the

MAGIC TREE HOUSE
RESEARCH GUIDES

The must-have, all-true companions for your
favorite Magic Tree House® adventures!